Haunted Hayride

##

Ready, Freddy!

Haunted Hayride

by ABBY KLEIN

illustrated by
JOHN McKINLEY

Scholastic Inc.

To Grady and Connor,
two little tricksters who love treats!
Happy Halloween!
Love, A.K.

ISBN 978-0-545-93172-4

10 9 8 7 6 5 4   16 17 18 19 20

Printed in the U.S.A   40

First printing, September 2016

CHAPTERS

I have a problem.

A really, really big problem.

The Halloween carnival is tonight, and everyone is going to go on the Haunted Hayride. I'm too afraid to go, but if I don't, then Max will call me a baby.

Let me tell you about it.

CHAPTER 1

The Bet

"I can't wait until tonight," I said to my best friend, Robbie, as I took a big bite of my turkey sandwich.

"Me either," he said.

Some mayonnaise dripped on my shirt, and I licked it off.

"The Halloween carnival does sound really awesome," said Josh. He was the new kid who had just moved here from California.

Josh took a grape, tossed it into the air,

opened his mouth, and the grape dropped right in. "Bull's-eye!" he yelled, pumping his fist in the air.

"That was so cool," I said. "Where did you learn to do that?"

"My dad taught me."

"Whatever," said Max. "Anyone can do that. It's not that big a deal."

"Oh really?" said Jessie. "Then let's see you try it."

"Even a baby can do it," said Max.

"Are you afraid to try it because you know you can't do it?" asked Josh.

"Who said I was afraid?" Max growled. "I'm not afraid of anything."

"Sure, sure," said Josh. "Blah, blah, blah. All you ever do is talk."

"I don't have any grapes, or else I'd show you right now," said Max.

"Here you go!" said Josh, throwing him one of his grapes. "Show us how easy it is."

"It should be really easy for someone with such a big mouth," I whispered to Robbie.

"Good one," Robbie said, laughing.

Max slowly turned his head in my direction and glared at me.

I gulped.

"What did you say?"

"I, uh . . . I, uh . . . ," I stammered.

"He said you have a really big mouth," Josh answered.

Oh no! "Why did you just tell him what I said?" I whispered to Josh. "Now I'm really going to get it."

Max jumped up out of his seat, reached across the table, and grabbed me by my T-shirt.

"Let go of him," said Josh.

"Says who?"

"Says me."

I gulped again.

Max twisted my shirt tighter.

"I said let go!" Josh yelled in Max's face.

Josh was so brave. Even though he was the new kid, he wasn't afraid to stand up to Max. He had a lot of guts. Max was the biggest bully in the whole first grade, and now he was the biggest bully in the whole second grade. Everyone was afraid of him. Everyone except Jessie and Josh.

"You heard him," Jessie yelled in Max's other ear. "Let Freddy go!"

Max looked from Josh to Jessie and back to Josh. Then he slowly let go of my shirt.

I stood there frozen for a minute. Then I carefully sat back down. "Thanks, guys," I whispered.

"No problem," said Josh. "You've got to stop being so afraid of him. He couldn't hurt a fly."

Jessie laughed. "You can say that again."

"So are you going to toss that grape into your mouth or not?" Josh asked Max.

Max grabbed the grape, threw it up in the air, and opened his big, fat mouth, but the grape hit him in the eye and bounced onto the floor.

"Ha, ha, ha, ha, ha!" Josh practically fell down on the floor, laughing.

"With aim like that, you won't win any games at the carnival tonight," said Jessie, giggling.

"A lot harder than it looks, huh, Max?" said Josh, getting back in his seat.

"I'll beat you at something tonight," Max mumbled. "Just you wait."

"Jessie, what's your favorite thing at the carnival?" asked Josh.

"The Haunted Hayride."

"The what?" asked Josh.

"The Haunted Hayride," Jessie repeated.

"What's that? It sounds spooky."

"It is!" said Jessie. "You go on a hayride in the woods behind school and monsters jump out and scare the pants off you!"

"Cool! I can't wait to go! Maybe we'll do that first."

"No," said Jessie. "You have to wait until it gets dark, really dark. That's when it's super fun."

"Awesome!" said Josh. "Freddy, we have to make sure we do that one together."

"Are you kidding?" said Max. "Freddy isn't going on the hayride."

"What do you mean?" asked Josh. "Of course Freddy is going."

"Oh no he's not," Max said, smirking.

"Why not?"

"Because he's a fraidy-cat. That's why."

"No he's not," said Josh. "No one is afraid of silly, old fake monsters in the dark. Right, Freddy?"

"I, um . . . I, um . . ."

"See. I told you," said Max. "He'll never go. He's too much of a baby."

"You don't know what you're talking about," said Josh. "He is not a baby. Of course Freddy is going on the Haunted Hayride."

"I bet he won't," said Max.

"Really?" said Josh. "I bet you he will. What do you want to bet?"

Robbie poked me in the ribs. "Tell him," he whispered. "You've got to tell Josh that you're too afraid to go."

"I can't do that," I whispered back.

"Why not?"

"Because I want Josh to be my friend. I don't want Josh to think I'm a wimp, and I don't want Max to go around telling everyone I'm a baby."

"Okay, here's the deal," said Max. "You have to give me one of your carnival prizes if Freddy doesn't go, and I have to give you one of mine if he does."

"I like it," said Josh. "It's a deal."

Max laughed. "I can't wait until tonight. I hope you win something good, just so I can take it away from you."

"You are not going to get any of my prizes," said Josh, "because Freddy is really brave. Just you wait and see."

"Oh, you'll be the one waiting," said Max. "You'll be waiting a long time, a very long time."

Josh put his arm around me. "You don't know what you're talking about, Max. Freddy isn't a fraidy-cat. Right, Freddy?"

"Right," I said, trying to sound strong but sounding more like a squeaky mouse.

CHAPTER 2

Monsters, Zombies, and Mummies

"So tell me more about this Haunted Hayride," Josh said on the bus ride home. "I never got to do anything like that at my school in California."

"You are going to love it," said Jessie.

"Did you say they take you in the woods behind school?" asked Josh.

"The deep, dark woods," said Jessie. "It's really creepy in there at night, and they set it up to look even creepier."

I pulled my hood up over my head to try to block out their conversation.

"First, they play this really creepy music."

"You mean the kind that sounds like ghosts moaning?" said Josh. "Ooo . . . ooo . . . ooo."

"Exactly," said Jessie. "The kind that sends chills up your spine."

Just listening to them was sending chills up my spine.

"Tell me more," said Josh.

Don't tell me more, I thought. I tried to cover my ears without looking too obvious.

Jessie continued, "The only light comes from a bunch of glowing jack-o'-lanterns that line the path."

"Did you say jack-o'-lanterns?" Chloe interrupted, jumping up out of her seat. "I love jack-o'-lanterns!"

"No one was talking to you," Max mumbled.

"But I don't like taking all of that gooey stuff out of the pumpkin," Chloe continued. "It's so messy and yucky." She made a face.

"That gooey stuff is called pulp," Robbie said.

"Well, whatever it's called, I think it's gross," said Chloe.

"Touching all of that slimy pulp is the best part of carving a pumpkin," said Jessie. "I love playing with all that goop."

Chloe wrinkled up her nose. "Well, I won't touch it. I make my daddy take it all out for me."

"Be quiet!" Max yelled. "No one cares."

Chloe scowled at Max and sank back down in her seat.

Josh shook his head. "Is she from another planet or what?"

Jessie laughed. "You'll get used to her after a while."

"Hey, Jessie," Josh continued, "didn't you say things reach out and grab you while you're on the hayride?"

"Oh yeah. You're just riding along, and then all of a sudden, something will jump out of the shadows and scream in your ear or grab you when you least expect it."

"Wow!" said Josh. "That sounds even cooler than I imagined."

It sounds even scarier than I imagined, I thought to myself. *I'll have nightmares for the rest of my life! There's no way I can go on this hayride.*

Robbie pulled my hood off my head and whispered in my ear. "Freddy."

"What?"

"Do you remember Chloe's Halloween party last year?"

I nodded my head. How could I forget?

"Remember how scared you were when stuff popped out of nowhere?"

I nodded again.

"I think you jumped, like, three feet in the air," said Robbie.

"I know. I know," I whispered. "Do you have to remind me?"

"So how do you think you're going to be able to go on a hayride in the woods? You don't even like to go for a walk in the woods at night."

He did have a point.

"Last summer when we went for a walk in the woods after dark to look for fireflies, you got totally freaked out when you heard an owl hooting. You thought it was a ghost, and you ran out of the woods, screaming."

I let out a big sigh. "What am I going to do?" I asked Robbie.

"Tell him," Robbie said.

"I can't do that." I pulled my hood back up over my head and closed my eyes. Why did I have to be so afraid of everything? If I don't go on that hayride, then Josh won't think I'm cool. I want to be a cool surfer kid just like him.

Josh poked me. "Freddy, I still can't believe Max bet me you wouldn't go on the Haunted Hayride."

I didn't answer.

"Freddy," Josh said tapping my head, "are you in there?"

I pulled my hood down.

"Sorry. Were you talking to me?"

"Yeah," said Josh, laughing. "I said, 'I can't believe Max bet me you wouldn't go on the Haunted Hayride.'"

"Uh . . . yeah . . . about that—" I started to say.

"This is going to be the easiest bet I've ever won in my life!" Josh said, still laughing.

Robbie elbowed me. "You'd better tell him," he whispered.

"I'm trying," I whispered back.

"I hope he wins a really great prize. I can't wait to see his face when I take it away from him."

"About that hayride—" I started to say again.

"It sounds so spooky," said Josh. "I just love when monsters and zombies and mummies come out of nowhere and totally surprise you when you least expect it."

Just listening to Josh talk about it was making me sick to my stomach.

"What's your favorite part?" Josh asked me.

"I don't know," I said.

"What do you mean you don't know?"

"I, uh . . . I, uh . . ."

"It's not a trick question, Freddy," Josh said.

"It kind of is for him," Robbie said.

"What do you mean? You guys are acting weird."

"Josh, I have something to tell you," I said.

"Okay, what is it?"

"I've never been on the Haunted Hayride," I whispered.

"Did you just say you've never been on the Haunted Hayride?" Josh yelled.

"Thanks for announcing it to the whole entire bus," I said.

"Oops, sorry," said Josh. "But is it true?" he whispered. "You've never been on it?"

I nodded. "Yep. It's true."

"But why not, Freddy?"

"Because . . . um . . . because . . . um," I stammered.

"Because why?"

"Because—" Robbie started to say, but I cut him off.

"Because my parents wouldn't let me," I lied.

Robbie turned and stared at me with a shocked expression on his face.

"Awesome!" said Josh. "Then it will be the first time for both of us."

"Yeah," I squeaked.

"I can't wait," said Josh, giving me a high five. "It's going to be the best night ever!"

"The best night ever!" I agreed. That is if I made it through the ride without throwing up in his lap.

CHAPTER 3

Two Things

If I was going to go on that hayride, then I was going to need two things: my lucky shark's tooth in my pocket and one of those neon glow-in-the-dark necklaces around my neck.

When I got home, I dashed upstairs to get my shark's tooth and put it in my pocket right then, so I wouldn't forget it later.

"Freddy? Is that you?" my mom called from downstairs.

"Yeah, Mom, it's me," I yelled back. "I'll be down in a little bit."

I ran into my room and opened my treasure box. I always keep my lucky shark's tooth in there, so it doesn't get lost.

"Where are you? Where are you?" I mumbled to myself as I rummaged around in the box.

"Ah! Here you are!" I said, smiling and holding up my shark's tooth. "You'd better bring me some good luck tonight and keep those monsters away." I gave it a kiss and shoved it deep into my pocket.

"Now I need the glow-in-the-dark necklace. I think I have one left over from the Fourth of July."

I sat down on the edge of my bed and hit my head with the palm of my hand. "Think, think, think. Where would it be? Maybe it's somewhere in my closet."

I went over to my closet, opened the door,

and started tossing things out . . . my Wiffle Ball bat . . . my Frisbee . . . my inflatable shark . . . my winter boots. "It's got to be in here somewhere," I said to myself.

"Freddy! Do you want a snack?" my mom yelled up again.

"No thanks. Not right now."

I kept searching through my closet, but I couldn't find the necklace anywhere. This was a problem, a big problem.

I know, I thought. *Maybe Suzie still has hers. We both got one at the Fourth of July parade.* Suzie never lets me borrow her things, but she'll never know it's her necklace unless I tell her. I just won't tell her, and then when the carnival is over, I'll put it back in her room where I found it.

I tiptoed to the top of the stairs. I could hear Suzie talking to Mom in the kitchen. *Good,* I thought. *I have some time before she comes upstairs, but I'd better hurry.*

I crept quietly into Suzie's room and looked around. Where would she keep a necklace like that?

I looked on her dresser where she has other necklaces and bracelets, but I didn't see it. Bummer. I just wanted to find it quickly and get out before she saw me.

Sometimes she keeps stuff like that in the drawer of her nightstand. I opened the drawer slowly because it usually creaks, but the necklace wasn't in there, either. I was running out of time.

I went over to her closet, opened the door, and stepped inside. Her closet was a lot neater than mine. It shouldn't be too hard to find what I was looking for.

I was so focused on what I was doing that I didn't hear Suzie come in the room. She snuck up behind me and yelled, "Boo!"

"AHHHHH!" I screamed, and jumped about three feet in the air. How was I going to go on a

Haunted Hayride if my own sister spooked me in her bedroom in the middle of the day?

When I turned around, Suzie was standing there with her hands on her hips, glaring at me. "What exactly do you think you're doing in my room?" she demanded.

"I, uh . . . I, uh . . ."

"You what?" she said. "Come on. Spit it out."

"I was looking for something."

"Well, you're not going to find it in *my* room," said Suzie.

"How do you know?" I said.

"Because everything in here is mine."

"I'm looking for my glow-in-the-dark necklace from the Fourth of July, and I think I found it," I said, holding up the necklace.

"That's mine," said Suzie.

"No it's not. It's mine."

"Is not."

"Is too."

"I know for a fact it's not yours," said Suzie.

"Oh really?" I said. "How do you know?"

"Because mine was red and yours was blue."

"I think mine was red," I said.

"No, Dad offered you the red one, but you threw a fit and said you had to have the blue one."

I knew the red one was hers. I was just hoping she had forgotten. "I don't think so," I said.

"I know so," Suzie said, grabbing it out of my hands. "So I'll just take it back right now."

Now what was I going to do?

"You can get out of my room now," Suzie said, waving her hand toward the door.

"Well . . . um," I said.

"Well, what?"

"I can't find my necklace, and I need one for the carnival tonight. Can I borrow yours?"

"Why do you need it for tonight?"

I ignored her and didn't answer.

Suzie held up her pinkie for a pinkie swear. "What's it worth to you?" she said.

I groaned. Why did she always have to do this? Why couldn't I borrow something from her just once without having to give her something in return? "Can't I just wear it tonight? I promise I'll give it back to you as soon as we get home."

"Sure you can wear it tonight," said Suzie.

"Really? Thanks so much!" I said, reaching for the necklace.

Suzie pulled her hand back. "Like I said, 'What's it worth to you?'" she said, holding up her pinkie once again.

I knew it was too good to be true. "I don't know," I said.

"Well, you'd better think of something, because I'm not just going to give you the necklace."

"How about I give you three pieces of my Halloween candy?"

"Three pieces?" Suzie said, laughing. "Are you kidding?"

"Five pieces?"

"How about six that I get to choose, and then I think we have a deal."

"Six! That you get to choose! Six pieces of candy for a dumb, old necklace?"

"If you think the necklace is so dumb, then I guess you don't need it."

"Fine, fine," I said, holding up my pinkie. "You can choose six pieces of my Halloween candy if you let me borrow the necklace tonight."

We locked our pinkies in a pinkie swear.

"Here you go," Suzie said, handing me the necklace.

"Thanks." I took the necklace and turned to leave.

"Hey, Freddy."

"What?"

"You never told me why you need the necklace."

"I just do," I mumbled, and walked out of her room.

CHAPTER 4

Beanbag Toss

On the car ride to the carnival, I could not stop thinking about the Haunted Hayride. I was usually really excited to go to the Halloween carnival, but not tonight. Tonight I wished I could skip it altogether. I didn't want to admit to Josh that I was too afraid to go on the ride.

"Freddy, are you all right?" my mom asked. "You're awfully quiet back there."

I didn't answer.

Suzie poked me. "Mom's talking to you, Sharkbreath."

"What? Huh? Did you say something to me, Mom?"

"Yes, honey. I said, are you all right?"

"Oh yeah, I'm fine."

"Well, you don't seem fine," said my dad. "Usually you can't stop talking about all the things you're going to do at the carnival."

I didn't want my parents to get suspicious, so I said, "I'm just trying to decide what I'm going to do first. Maybe I'll do the Beanbag Toss, or the Balloon Burst, or the Gone Fishin', or . . ."

"Wait a minute," said my mom. "Did you say Gone Fishin'?"

"Yes, he did," said Suzie.

"Is that the one where you win a live goldfish if you get a paper fish with an X on its back?"

"Yep, that's the one," I said.

"You think Mom is going to let you have a pet fish?" said Suzie, laughing. "Think again."

"Of course she will," I said. "Right, Mom?"

"Now, Freddy, you know how I feel about

any kind of animals in the house," said my mom.

"But, Mom, fish are not like dogs. They don't bark, and they don't shed fur."

"Good try," whispered Suzie, "but she's still going to say no."

"I'm sorry, Freddy, but I'm still going to have to say no to a fish."

"Told you so," said Suzie.

"Come on, Mom," I pleaded. "Pretty please with a cherry on top? I'm older now, so I can take care of it by myself."

"Freddy, your mother said no, so the answer is no," said my dad.

"It's not fair," I mumbled, and stuck out my lower lip.

Just then we pulled into the school parking lot. "Here we are!" said my dad. "Freddy, let's turn that frown upside down."

"Time for some fun," said my mom.

Suzie and I jumped out of the car.

"I told Kimberly that I'd meet her at the tie-dye booth. See you guys later," said Suzie as she disappeared into the crowd.

I had just entered the carnival when someone came up behind me and yelled, "Boo!"

I jumped.

"Ha-ha! Did I scare you, Freddy?" said Josh. "Just getting you ready for the Haunted Hayride later."

Did he have to remind me? I was hoping he was going to forget about the hayride, but apparently not.

"Cool necklace," said Josh. "I like how it glows red like vampire blood. Where'd you get it?"

"I didn't get it here," I said. "I got it at a Fourth of July parade."

"Do you want to go play some games with me?" asked Josh.

"Sure!" I said. Maybe playing games would get my mind off how nervous I was about the hayride.

"What do you want to play first?" asked Josh.

"Let's go do the Beanbag Toss," I said. "I'm usually pretty good at that, and I want to win some prizes."

We took off running toward the games. "See you later, Mom and Dad!" I called over my shoulder.

"Be careful!" my mom yelled. "Have fun!"

When we got to the Beanbag Toss, Jessie was already in line. Josh snuck up behind her and yelled, "Boo!"

Jessie didn't even flinch. She just laughed.

"Hey, Jessie," said Josh.

"Hey, guys. I was hoping I would find you here."

"Jessie is really good at this game," I said.

"Really?" said Josh.

"Yeah," I said. "Jessie is the pitcher on our baseball team."

"A girl pitcher. Wow! That's cool," said Josh.

"Thanks," Jessie said, smiling.

"And she has a really good arm," I said. "Wait until you see her throw the beanbag."

"Looks like I won't have to wait long," said Josh. "It's Jessie's turn now."

For the Beanbag Toss there was a picture of a witch painted on a wooden board, but there was a hole cut out where the witch's mouth would have been. You had to throw the beanbags through the hole. If you got all three of them in, then you won a prize.

Jessie picked up the first beanbag, took aim, and threw it hard toward the witch's mouth.

"Bull's-eye!" Josh yelled. "That's one!"

Jessie picked up the second one and once again tossed it right through the hole.

"Wow! You weren't kidding, Freddy," said Josh. "Jessie really does have a great arm."

"That's two," said the lady in the booth. "You only need one more, honey, to win a prize."

"Come on, Jessie, you can do it," I shouted, clapping my hands.

Jessie whipped the third beanbag, and it whizzed right in.

"Three!" yelled Josh. "You got all three!"

Jessie had a big grin on her face. "Easy peasy," she said.

"You get to pick a prize," said the lady. "What would you like?"

"Can I have one of those orange spider rings, please?" said Jessie.

"Sure thing, honey," said the lady, handing it to Jessie. "Here you go."

Jessie put the ring on.

"That's cool and creepy," said Josh. "Freddy, let's try to win one of those, too, so we can all have one."

"Good idea," I said. "It can be like a secret spider club."

"You go first," said Josh.

I quickly threw my first, then my second, and then my third beanbag, and they all went in. "Oh yeah! Oh yeah! Oh yeah!" I sang as I danced around. "I did it! I did it! I did it!"

Jessie giggled. "You look like a dancing chicken," she said.

"I'd like a green spider ring please," I told the lady. "Your turn now, Josh."

"Josh, Josh, Josh," Jessie and I chanted.

Josh picked up the beanbags. "There's one! There's two! There's three!" he said as he hurled them through the air.

"Woo-hoo! You did it!" Jessie and I shouted. "You got them all in."

"I'd like the black spider ring, please," said Josh.

Just then a voice said, "Really? A black spider ring? That's so lame."

I'd know that voice anywhere. It was Max.

"Josh, you're going to have to win better prizes than that tonight," said Max, "so when I win our little bet I get to take something really good away from you. Something like this," said Max, holding up a clear plastic bag with a real live goldfish swimming around in it.

CHAPTER 5

Gone Fishin'

"Is that a real goldfish?" Josh asked Max.

"Of course it's real. Can't you see it swimming around?" said Max, shoving the bag into Josh's face.

"That's awesome! I can't wait to take that away from you when I win the bet," said Josh.

I wished the two of them would stop talking about the bet. It was making my stomach hurt.

Just then Robbie came running up. "Hey, guys, I've been looking all over for you. What's up?"

"I was just telling Max that he's going to have to give me that goldfish later, when Freddy goes on the hayride and I win the bet," said Josh.

"Ha-ha! That's funny that you think you're going to win," said Max. "I *know* I'm going to win because I know Freddy way better than you do, and he's afraid of everything . . . and I mean *everything*!"

"I know I'm new around here," said Josh, "but Freddy seems like a pretty tough kid to me."

I smiled to myself. Josh, the cool surfer dude from California, thinks I'm tough.

"Well, you'd better go win your own goldfish, because you are definitely not going to get mine," Max said as he turned and walked away.

"We'll see about that!" Josh called after him.

"What should we do now?" Jessie asked.

"I really want one of those goldfish," said Josh. "Don't you, Freddy?"

"I wish," I said.

"Then let's go play Gone Fishin'," said Josh.

"I can't."

"What do you mean you can't?"

"Freddy's mom is a neat freak," said Robbie. "She won't let him have any animals in the house."

"But fish aren't like other animals," said Josh. "They don't bring mud into the house. You don't have to clean up their poop."

"I know. I know," I said. "I've tried telling her all of that, but it's no use. No animals, period."

"Wow! That's a bummer," said Josh.

"Do you have any pets?" asked Robbie.

"Yeah, I have a dog named Yogi. He's awesome. He even sleeps on my bed at night," said Josh.

"I am so jealous!" I said. "I really want a dog that sleeps on my bed."

"Robbie, do you have any pets?"

"Robbie has, like, a whole zoo at his house!" I said. "He has all kinds of pets."

"Really?" said Josh.

"You'll have to come over and see them sometime," said Robbie.

"I'd love to," said Josh. "Maybe one day after school."

"Sure thing," said Robbie.

"I have one goldfish named Choopy," said Jessie, "and I'd like to give her a friend, so let's go fishing!"

We all ran over to the Gone Fishin' booth.

Robbie, Josh, and Jessie all got in line.

"Aren't you going to play?" said Josh. "Just for the fun of it."

"No. That's okay. I'll just watch you guys," I said.

The guy in the booth handed them each a fishing pole with a magnet on the end. They had to drop the fishing line behind a curtain painted to look like the ocean. The magnet would "catch" a paper fish that each player had to reel in. If the paper fish had a big X on it, they'd win a real goldfish.

Jessie went first. She threw her fishing line over the curtain.

"I think you've caught one," the guy said. "Go ahead and reel it in."

"Come on, come on," Jessie whispered to herself as she reeled the fish in. "I want a friend for Choopy."

"Did you win? Did you win?" Josh asked.

"I don't know. I haven't looked yet," said Jessie as she pulled the paper fish off the end of the line. Slowly, she turned the fish over in her hand, and there on the back was a big black *X*. "I won! I won!" Jessie shouted, jumping up and down.

"Way to go!" said Josh.

"It's your lucky night," I said, giving her a high five.

"Here you go," said the guy as he handed Jessie her fish in a bag. "Be careful and take good care of it."

"Thanks, I will!" said Jessie.

"What are you going to name it?" I asked.

"I'm not sure yet," said Jessie. "I have to think about it. Maybe Pessy."

"Bessie? Rhymes with Jessie?"

"No, Pessy."

"Pessy? What kind of name is that?" I said.

"Well, *pescado* means 'fish' in Spanish, so I thought I could call him Pessy for short."

"That's cool," said Josh. "I like it."

Robbie went next. He threw his fishing pole into the ocean, caught a fish, reeled it in, pulled his fish off the line, and looked at the back.

"Bummer," said Robbie. "No *X*."

"Sorry, dude," said Josh.

"Better luck next time," I said, patting Robbie on the back.

"Your turn, Josh," said Jessie. "Good luck!"

The guy handed him a fishing pole.

"You know," said Josh, "the beach was only a few blocks from my house in California. If I win a fish and keep it in my bedroom, maybe I won't miss the ocean so much."

Josh tossed his fishing line to catch a fish and then reeled it in.

"I can't look. I'm too nervous," said Josh. "Freddy, would you check it out for me and tell me if I won?"

"You want me to look?" I said.

"Yeah," said Josh. "Take the fish off the line and tell me if it has a black *X* on it."

I carefully pulled the paper fish off the line. I think I was just as nervous as Josh was.

"Come on, look already!" said Robbie. "The suspense is killing me."

My heart was beating really fast. I slowly turned the fish over . . .

"Did I win?" asked Josh. "Is there a black *X*?"

I shook my head. "Sorry," I said. "No *X*."

"You can always try again," said the guy in the booth.

"Or I can just take Max's fish when I win that bet tonight," Josh said, smiling. "Right, Freddy?"

I gulped and pretended to laugh. "Ha-ha! Right."

CHAPTER 6

Hot Dog Vampires

"So, what should we do now?" asked Jessie.

"I don't know about you guys, but I'm starving," said Robbie. "I think we should go get something to eat."

"Great idea!" said Josh. "My stomach is growling. Freddy, what do you want to eat?"

My stomach was growling, too, but not because I was hungry. I was so worried about that hayride that I didn't really feel like eating anything. "I don't know," I said.

"Let's go over to the food area and see what they've got," said Jessie.

We all walked over to the food trucks.

"Wow!" said Josh. "They've got so many choices: hot dogs, hamburgers, tacos, pizza, chicken fingers, sandwiches . . . I don't know what to choose."

"I know what I want," said Jessie.

"Let me guess," I said. "Tacos."

Jessie laughed. "Yep. I'm going to get tacos. You know I love tacos."

"I love tacos, too," said Josh.

"You do?" said Jessie.

"Yeah, I used to eat them all the time in California. There is a place called the Taco Hut that makes the best tacos in the world."

"Actually, my *abuela*, my grandma, makes the best tacos in the world," said Jessie. "She's from Mexico, and she has a secret recipe that she has been using since she was a little girl."

"Freddy, have you ever had her tacos?" Josh asked.

"Of course! They are sooooooo good," I said, licking my lips.

"Josh, you'll have to come over and try them some time," said Jessie.

"For sure!" said Josh. "Thanks, Jessie."

"I think I might get a hot dog," said Robbie.

"We could all get hot dogs and be hot dog vampires," said Josh.

"Hot dog vampires? What's that?" I asked.

"You don't know what a hot dog vampire is?" said Josh. "Come on. Let's get hot dogs and I'll show you."

The three of us got hot dogs, and Jessie got some tacos.

"Now get a knife and some ketchup," said Josh, "and meet me at that table over there."

Robbie and I got what we needed and joined Josh and Jessie at the table.

"Now what?" asked Robbie.

"First, you have to make your fangs," said Josh.

"How do we do that?" I asked.

"You cut a small chunk off each end of the hot dog, like this," Josh said as he cut his pieces off and held them up for us to see.

Robbie and I did exactly what he did.

"These are going to be our fangs."

"Now what?" said Robbie.

"Now you dip each of the pieces into ketchup, so it looks like our fangs are dripping with blood."

We dipped our pretend fangs into the ketchup.

"Freddy, you need to dip yours a little more," said Josh. "You want them to look really bloody."

All this talk of bloody fangs was not making me feel any better. In fact, it was making me feel worse!

"Do I have enough blood on mine?" Robbie asked.

"Yeah," said Josh. "That's perfect. Now you push the pieces of hot dog over your two top front teeth like this," Josh continued as he put his fangs in place.

Robbie copied Josh and shoved the hot dog pieces onto his teeth. Then, in his best vampire voice, he said, "I vant to suck your blood."

It was hilarious! We all burst out laughing.

"Come on, Freddy. You try it," said Josh.

I pushed my fangs in place and started to say, "I vant to suck—" but before I could finish, one of my fangs dropped onto the table.

We all burst out laughing again.

"What's so funny?" Chloe asked as she came walking up to our table.

Josh leaned over close to Chloe's neck and said, "Come here, little girl. I vant to suck your blood."

Chloe jumped back, screaming, "Ewww! Ewww! Ewww!"

"Ha, ha, ha!" Josh laughed.

"You all are so gross," said Chloe.

"It's only hot dogs and ketchup," said Josh.

"Well, my mama says you should never play with your food."

"Well, my mom was the one who taught me how to be a hot dog vampire," said Josh.

I picked up my fang that had dropped onto the table and offered it to Chloe. "Here, do you want to try being a hot dog vampire?"

"Was that already in your mouth?" she asked.

"Yep," I said.

"And it's got his saliva all over it," said Robbie.

"DIS-GUS-TING!" said Chloe. "You are all pigs."

"No, they are all vampires," Jessie said, grinning.

"Ugh!" said Chloe, sticking her nose in the air. "I can't stay here anymore and watch you play with your food." She turned and started to walk away.

"That's too bad," Josh called after her. "You're missing out on all the fun."

"Later, Miss Fancypants!" Jessie shouted.

"Is she always like that?" Josh asked.

"Always," the three of us answered and then laughed.

I was having such a good time, I had almost forgotten about the hayride. That is until I heard that voice again.

"What's so funny?"

I didn't even have to turn around to know it was Max.

"We're pretending to be vampires," said Josh.

"That's so lame," said Max.

"It's not lame," said Josh. "It's actually pretty fun. Do you want to try it?"

Josh always knew the right thing to say to Max. He was never intimidated by him. I wish I could be like that. I wish I could stand up to the biggest bully in the whole second grade and not be afraid of him.

"I don't want to play your baby games," said Max. "I just came to see if you've won any other good prizes."

"Nope. Just my spider ring," Josh said, shoving the ring into Max's face.

Max swatted Josh's hand away. "I don't want that, so you'd better get busy winning some cooler stuff. Why don't you go do the Cake Walk and win that awesome Frankenstein cake, just so I can take it away from you."

"Oh! The Cake Walk! I almost forgot

about it," said Jessie. "Thanks for reminding us, Max. Come on, guys. Finish up your hot dogs. You don't want to miss the Cake Walk, Josh."

"Yeah, you don't want to miss it," Max said, grinning.

CHAPTER 7

Cake Walk

Jessie shoved the last bite of taco into her mouth and took off running.

We gobbled up our hot dogs and sprinted after her.

"Wow! She's fast!" said Josh.

"She's one of the fastest kids in the whole school," I said.

"Hurry up, guys!" Jessie shouted. "It's about to start."

Huffing and puffing, we finally caught up to her.

"Whew!" said Josh, panting. "I need a minute to catch my breath."

"Me, too!" I said. "Jessie, you're fast as lightning."

Jessie smiled. "Come over here, guys. These cakes all look so good. I don't know which one to pick if I win."

"Look at this one," said Robbie. "It looks just like a haunted house, and it has marshmallow ghosts flying out of the windows."

"I like this one," I said, pointing to a big, orange jack-o'-lantern cake. "The teeth are made out of candy corn, and I love candy corn!"

"Ooo, ooo, come over here," said Jessie. "Look at this. It's a witch. Her whole face is made out of green M&M'S ... those are my favorite!"

"Josh, which one do you like?" Robbie asked.

"This Frankenstein one *is* really cool."

Just then Max walked up. "Told you so," he said, grinning. "But you're never going to win it because I am."

"We'll see about that," said Josh.

"Okay, everybody, come over here," said the lady at the Cake Walk booth. "I'm going to tell you the rules."

"Good," said Josh, "because I've never done a Cake Walk before."

"You haven't?" I said. "You're kidding."

"Nope. Never."

"Well, it's really fun, and if you win, you get a whole cake!"

"Okay, listen up," said the lady.

Just then Chloe came skipping over to us, waving her hands in the air and screaming, "Wait! Wait for me! You can't start without me!"

"Yes we can!" said Max.

"No you can't!"

"Oh yes we can!"

"Oh no you can't!"

The lady interrupted them. "Are the two of you done arguing yet? Can I go over the rules now?"

"Yes," said Chloe, fluffing up her red curls. "I'm ready now."

"Okay. Rule number one: no running or skipping. You have to walk the whole time."

"But I love to skip," Chloe whined.

"Well, you'll have to do it some other time," said the lady. "Rule number two: no pushing. If you push someone out of a seat, then you will be disqualified."

"Did you hear that, Max?" Josh yelled. "No pushing."

Max scowled at Josh.

The lady continued, "When the music starts, you walk around the circle of chairs. When the music stops, sit down in the closest chair. If that chair has a picture of a cake taped to the bottom, then you get to choose one of these delicious cakes to take home."

Josh turned to me. "That's it? That's all I have to do?"

"That's it," I said, smiling.

"I just have to sit my butt down on a chair with a cake picture taped on the bottom?"

"Easy, right?"

"Easy peasy lemon squeezy," said Josh.

"Is there only one winner?" Jessie asked.

"No, we'll keep going until we get three winners," said the lady.

"I will definitely be one of them," said Max.

"In your dreams," said Josh. "In your *dreams*."

Max glared at Josh.

"Is everybody ready?" said the lady.

"Ready!" we all said.

The music started, and we all began moving in a circle around the chairs. We walked around about three times, and I was beginning to wonder if she was ever going to turn off the music, when all of a sudden, the music stopped.

I dropped down into the closest chair.

"Okay, everybody, look under your chair and see if there's a picture of a cake."

"I won! I won!" Chloe shouted. She pulled the picture of the cake off the bottom of her chair, and then she stood on the chair and yelled, "Look, everybody! Look! I'm a winner!"

"Look, everybody! Look! I'm a winner!" Max said in a squeaky voice, imitating Chloe.

Chloe put her hands on her hips. "Stop copying me."

Max put his hands on *his* hips. "Stop copying me."

"Those two are crazy," said Josh, circling his finger next to his ear to make the cuckoo sign.

"Would you please come down off that chair," said the lady. "I don't want you to fall."

Chloe carefully stepped down off the chair.

"Which cake would you like, honey?"

"I want this beautiful princess one," said Chloe, "because I am a beautiful princess."

"Oh brother," Jessie whispered to me and rolled her eyes.

The music started again, and once again, we all started moving around the circle. This time I think we went around only once when the music stopped.

"Check your chairs!" shouted the lady.

We all bent down to look.

Jessie started jumping up and down. "Look, guys! Look! I got a lucky chair! I win a cake!"

"You're so lucky," I said, smiling.

"Which one would you like?" asked the lady.

"Heh, heh, heh," Jessie cackled. "I'd like the witch, please."

The lady handed her the cake. Jessie licked her lips. "I can't wait to eat a big piece of this later."

"All right, this is your last chance," said the lady.

"I *know* I'm going to win this time," said Max.

"How do you know?" said Josh.

"I just know," Max said, grinning.

The music started, and we walked around and around and around. It seemed like forever. Then the music stopped. Max and Josh had stopped right next to each other.

Josh was about to sit in a chair when Max yelled, "That's my chair!" and shoved Josh so hard that he fell to the ground.

The lady came running over. "Are you all right?" she asked Josh.

"Yeah, I'm fine."

"You, young man, are disqualified," she said, pointing to Max.

"That's not fair," Max whined.

"Oh yes it is," said the lady. "You broke the rules. You pushed."

Josh got up off the ground and sat in the chair.

"Now you may all check your chairs," said the lady.

Josh slowly peeked under his chair. "No way! No way!" he shouted. "I won! I won!"

"Congratulations," said the lady. "Which cake would you like?"

Josh looked right at Max. "I'll take the Frankenstein cake, please."

"That's so not fair!" said Max. "That cake should be mine!"

"Maybe it would have been if you played by the rules," said the lady.

"Too bad. So sad," Josh said to Max.

"You're going to be the sad one in about an hour when the Haunted Hayride is over, and you've lost the bet," said Max. "Because I am going to take that cake away from you."

"I think the hayride starts in about ten minutes," said Jessie. "We'd better leave our cakes here for now and get over there so we don't miss it!"

"We definitely don't want to miss it!" said Josh.

Oh no! The Haunted Hayride. I had forgotten all about it.

They all took off running. Everyone except me. I couldn't move. I felt like my feet were cemented to the ground.

"Hey, Freddy!" Josh called over his shoulder. "Are you coming or what?"

"Uh, yeah! Coming!" I yelled. That is, if I could get my feet to move and I didn't throw up.

CHAPTER 8

The Haunted Hayride

I wondered if the bet would be off if I didn't make it to the hayride in time. I could pretend that I had to go to the bathroom really badly and stay in there just long enough so that by the time I got back, the ride had already left. *Yes, that's a great plan*, I thought. No one would ever know that I was too afraid to go.

I started to run toward the bathroom, but then Josh appeared out of nowhere and grabbed me by the arm. "There you are, Freddy!" he said, and started pulling me in the direction of the woods. "Come on!"

"I'll be there in a minute," I said. "I just have to go to the bathroom first."

"There's no time for that!" Josh yelled, dragging me closer to the woods. "You'll just have to hold it."

Oh no! My bathroom plan was ruined. What was I going to do now?

We were getting closer and closer to the ride, and my heart was beating faster and faster. "I can't do it," I mumbled to myself.

"Did you say something?" asked Josh.

I stopped running. "I have something to tell you," I said.

"Can it wait until after the ride?" asked Josh. "I don't want to miss it."

"Uh, not really," I said. "I have to tell you now."

"Okay," said Josh. "What is it?"

"I don't think I can go on the Haunted Hayride."

"Why not?"

"Because . . . because . . ."

"Because why?"

"You promise you won't laugh at me?"

"I promise," said Josh.

"Because I'm too afraid to go," I whispered. There, I said it.

"Well, why didn't you just say so?" said Josh.

"Because I wanted you to be my friend. I didn't want you to think I was a baby."

"I don't think you're a baby," said Josh. "I think you're a really cool kid."

"Really?"

"Really," said Josh.

"Well, Max thinks I'm a baby, and if I don't go on the ride, then he's going to tell everyone I'm a fraidy-cat and a baby."

"I have an idea," said Josh.

"You do?"

"Yeah. What if I let you borrow my good

luck charm? Would that make you feel less scared?"

"You have a good look charm?" I said, surprised. "I have one, too!"

Josh reached into his pocket and pulled out a shark's tooth. "Here's my good luck charm."

My mouth dropped open. "No way!" I was shocked. "My lucky charm is also a shark's tooth!"

We both laughed.

"I guess we were meant to be friends," said Josh.

"I guess so," I said, smiling.

"Well, with two shark teeth in your pocket, there's no way you'll get scared," said Josh, handing me his tooth.

"Thanks," I said, sticking his tooth deep into my pocket.

"We'd better get going," said Josh. "We don't want to miss the ride."

"No, we don't," I said.

The two of us took off running and made it to the ride just in time.

"Well, look who's here," said Max. "What took you so long? Were you trying to convince the little baby to go?"

"No way!" said Josh. "Freddy didn't need any convincing."

"Just remember," said Max. "He has to make it through the whole ride for you to win the bet."

"No problem," said Josh. "Right, Freddy?"

I nodded.

Max frowned.

Josh and I jumped onto the wagon and sat down next to Robbie and Jessie.

"Are you going to be able to do this?" Robbie asked.

"I think so," I said, sticking my hand in my pocket and rubbing the two lucky shark teeth.

"It's really dark out here," said Jessie. "Good thing you wore that glow-in-the-dark necklace, Freddy."

It was definitely worth giving up six pieces of Halloween candy, I thought to myself.

"Is everybody ready?" said a spooky voice.

I looked up and saw that the guy driving the hay cart had on a really scary mask. I shivered.

Josh leaned over and whispered, "It's just a guy in a mask."

"It's just a guy in a mask," I muttered to myself. "It's just a guy in a mask."

The ride started, and that spooky, ghostly music began floating through the air. "OOOOOEEEEEEOOOOO."

We entered the woods, and it was pitch-black. You couldn't see a thing. I wrapped my arms around my body and squeezed myself tight.

"Oh, look at baby Freddy," said Max. "I think he needs his mommy."

"Leave him alone," said Josh. "He's fine."

"Are you sure you don't want to get off?" said Max.

I ignored him.

All of a sudden, a zombie jumped out of the woods and grabbed Josh's leg.

My heart skipped a few beats, and I wanted to scream, but Josh just started laughing.

"Ha, ha, ha! That was awesome!" he said. Then he leaned over to me and whispered, "See, Freddy. There's nothing to be scared of."

Next a monster popped out from behind a tree and growled in Jessie's ear, "GRRRRRR!"

Jessie clapped her hands and yelled, "More! More!"

Then out of nowhere a werewolf pretended to eat me and howled, "OW-OW-OW-OWOOOOO!"

Instead of screaming, I started to laugh . . . and then I couldn't stop laughing.

"You're not supposed to be laughing," said Max. "You're supposed to be crying."

"Looks like someone is going to lose a bet," said Josh.

Max crossed his arms and stuck out his lower lip.

We continued riding through the woods for a while, being attacked by ghosts and zombies, mummies and werewolves, vampires and monsters.

"Is it over already?" I asked when the ride finally came to a stop.

"Way to go!" Josh said, giving me a high five. "You did it!"

"Thanks," I whispered.

"No problem," said Josh. "That's what friends are for."

We all jumped down off the ride.

Max started to walk away.

"Hold on there, dude," said Josh. "Hand over that goldfish."

Max just stood there with the goldfish in his hand.

"If I won, you had to give me one of your carnival prizes," said Josh. "Freddy went on the hayride, so I won. Now give me that fish."

Max grunted, handed over the fish, and stomped away.

"Better luck next time," Josh called after him.

We all laughed.

"Well, Freddy," said Josh. "You were awesome, and because you were so brave, I now have a new ocean friend to remind me of California. You'll have to come over to my house sometime soon and visit him."

"I'd like that," I said. "I'd really like that."

"Now let's all go eat some cake!" said Jessie, and we all took off chanting, "Cake, cake, cake!"

Freddy's Fun Pages

HALLOWEEN WORD SEARCH

Find each of these Halloween words hidden in the word search. The words may be vertical, horizontal, diagonal, or even backward. Circle the word when you find it.

```
P R M Y M M U M E N V N
W E R E W O L F E A I E
G T N P Y E Q E M K S I
H S K O C X W P P J S B
O N T L M O I M B F E M
S O E O L R U C N Y C O
T M R L E P S V J Y N Z
F R A N K E N S T E I N
S H W I T C H D W Q R H
H A U N T E D D B Z P F
```

HALLOWEEN MUMMY GHOST VAMPIRE
FRANKENSTEIN WITCH ZOMBIE PRINCESS
MONSTER HAUNTED PUMPKIN WEREWOLF

HIDDEN WORDS

Freddy found the word EAR hidden in
the word HAYRIDE.
How many words can you spell using the
letters in the word HAYRIDE?
(You can only use each letter once in
each word.)

HAYRIDE

_____

_____

_____

_____

_____

MONSTER SLIME

Freddy loves to make Monster Slime at Halloween time! To make some slime of your own, use Freddy's recipe below.

Ingredients:

1 teaspoon of Borax powder

1 ½ cups of water, divided

4 ounces (or ½ cup) Elmer's glue—you can use clear or white (ask an adult to help with this part!)

Green food coloring

Directions:

1. Fill a small bowl with 1 cup of water and add 1 teaspoon of Borax powder. Mix until the Borax is dissolved and set aside.
2. Pour glue into a medium mixing bowl and add ½ cup of water.

3. Add four drops of food coloring to the glue mixture.

4. Stir it up a little bit and then add the Borax mixture to the glue mixture. Watch it begin to solidify.

5. Mix it up with your hands.

6. Pour out the excess water and knead the mixture until it becomes firm and dry.

7. Have fun playing with your slime!

8. When you are done playing with it, store it in a Ziploc bag or airtight container.